The Seven Golden Apples

Robert Cirillo

ISBN 978-0-9978807-3-1

Photographs of Amantea by Vicente Mauriziano and Robert Cirillo
Photographs of the Allan children by Irma C. Lua-Allan
Illustrations designed by Robert Cirillo and carried out by Mike Motz

For requests for permission to reproduce, contact:

Robert Cirillo
ciril000@planet.nl

Windjammer Adventure Publishing
289 South Franklin Street, Chagrin Falls, OH 44022
Telephone 440.247.6610 Email windjammerpub@mac.com

The Seven Golden Apples

I setti puma d'oru

Le sette mele d'oro

Author's preface

The story of *The Seven Golden Apples* has been in my family for at least five generations. My great grandfather, Gaetano Caruso, born in the town of Amantea in the Italian Region of Calabria in 1873, told the story to my father around 1930 when my father was a boy. My father shared the story with his six children and we have shared it with our descendants. The title of the story in Italian is *Le sette mele d'oro*, but in the language spoken by my great grandfather, Calabrese, it is *I setti puma d'oru*.

I attempted to trace the story to its origins. I interviewed quite a number of people in Calabria, but I did not find anyone who could remember the story of *The Seven Golden Apples*. The reader can imagine how I felt telling the story in Italian in Calabria. I felt that I was bringing the story home after more than a hundred thirty years!

In my search for the origins of the story I also spent considerable time in Italian bookstores and on the Internet searching for and reading Italian folktales. I read literally hundreds of them, but did not find the story of the *Seven Golden Apples* as told by my great grandfather. Interestingly, I did discover a number of stories whose plot contained striking similarities to the story of *The Seven Golden Apples*, but none of them were identical to it. For readers who may be interested, some of the better examples of stories whose plot overlaps to some extent with that of *The Seven Golden Apples* are *Il drago dalle sette teste* (*The Dragon with Seven Heads),* published by Italo Calvino; *Baffidirame* (*Copper-Colored Mustache*), published by Giuseppe Gabutti; *Il mago dalle sette teste* (*The Sorcerer with Seven Heads*) by Giuseppe Pitrè; *Il conto delle mele d'oro* (*The Story of the Golden Apples*) by Giambattista Basile; and *The Three Golden Apples*, which is included in *Tuscan Fairy Tales,* published by Vernon Lee. I should also mention that in Greek mythology one of the twelve labors of Hercules (the eleventh) is the theft of the golden apples from the garden of the Hesperides, but this has nothing to do with the golden apples in the folktale in this book. My conclusion is that it is very possible that my great grandfather truly was the author of the story, although he most probably borrowed plot elements from other folktales.

It is not easy to take a story that has always been handed down orally and put it into written form, but I thoroughly enjoyed the challenge. A great many adaptations were necessary. For example, I added a lot of details and embellishments to the story and applied literary techniques and characterization that were not present in the original oral version. In order to give my readers an idea of the extent of my embellishments, when my father at the request of his children finally put the story in writing, he only needed six typed pages! Compare that with the length of this book! Nonetheless, everything that was in the original oral version is present in my written version, and whereas I have done a lot of embellishing,

I have changed nothing.

The titles of the chapters of the story are trilingual in English, Calabrese and Italian.

It is a great honor and pleasure for me to be able to make known to the world a piece of Southern Italian culture that is also an important part of my family's history.

Dedications

This book is dedicated first and foremost to my great grandfather, Gaetano Caruso, the apparent originator of the story. Gaetano Caruso was born in the town of Amantea in the Italian Region of Calabria in 1873.

Gaetano Caruso

The book is also dedicated to my father, Joseph Anthony Cirillo, from whom I first heard the story. My father was born in 1924 in Springfield, Massachusetts.

Joseph Anthony Cirillo

Joseph Anthony Cirillo

8

Joseph Anthony Cirillo (middle) and Gaetano Caruso (right)

I also dedicate the book to Michelle and Jennifer Allan, whose enthusiastic reaction to the story of *The Seven Golden Apples* was an essential motivating factor in my deciding to write it down.

Michelle Allan, Robert Cirillo and Jennifer Allan

Finally, I dedicate the book to the people of Amantea who helped me discover interesting things about my family's history, especially Vicente Mauriziano, Roberto Musì and Giuseppe (Peppe) Marchese.

Amantea, Calabria

Amantea, Calabria

Amantea, Calabria

PUMARIA

The Seven Golden Apples
I setti puma d'oru
Le sette mele d'oro

I. Pumaria

Once upon a time in a far-away land there lived a benevolent king named Giuseppe. His kingdom was bordered on the north, east and west by a vast, treacherous mountain range and on the south by a large mediterranean sea. In the eastern part of the kingdom, extending into the foothills of the mountain range, was a large forest that provided not only lumber for building but also nuts, berries and wild game such as deer and wild boar. On the western edge of the kingdom, on the edge of the foothills of the mountain range, were quarries from which stone was extracted for the purpose of building. The central part of the kingdom, extending from the mountains to the sea, was a fertile valley. There were also rivers and streams flowing swiftly from the surrounding mountains all the way to the sea. They were abundant with fish and also kept the fertile land well irrigated and ideal for farming. There was always plenty of food to keep the inhabitants of Giuseppe's kingdom well fed.

The summers in the kingdom were warm and the winters were mild. This climate was favorable for the cultivation of many types of grains, fruits and vegetables, but of all the things that grew in the kingdom the most special were the apples. Because of the great number of apple trees throughout the land, it became known as the Kingdom of Pumaria. (In the language spoken in Giuseppe's kingdom *pumu* was the word for *apple*.) The apple trees in Pumaria were considerably taller than apple trees found in other lands, sometimes reaching a height of thirty feet. It was very possible that the largest, sweetest, juiciest apples in the whole world grew there. Apples from Pumaria were easy to recognize. They were bright yellow in color. In fact, the yellow color of Pumarian apples was so deep and rich that the apples appeared to be made of gold.

King Giuseppe, because he was wise and just, inspired loyalty among his subjects and thus succeeded in creating a productive, thriving civilization. He took advantage of the long coastline of his kingdom to establish three ports from which he exported merchandise by ship to the lands on the other side of the sea. Of all the items exported from Pumaria, the sweet, gold-colored apples were the highest in demand.

All travel and commerce took place via the sea because the Kingdom of Pumaria was completely inaccessible except by way of the coast. No one had ever been known to reach Pumaria by way of the mountains that surrounded the kingdom. In fact, no one ever ventured into the mountains at all because they evoked feelings of fear and foreboding in everyone. There were many frightening legends about the mountains, and many of those legends dated all the way back to the time when Pumaria was first settled, before the kingdom of Giuseppe had even been established. They had been passed down from generation to generation and were still an important part of the folklore of Pumaria. They told of narrow, treacherous paths along high cliffs, of dangerous caves, of pits hidden by dense undergrowth, of peaks so high that they were covered with snow and ice, of ferocious wild

beasts and even of monsters. Several curses were associated with the mountains. In the early years of the reign of Giuseppe a brave explorer would occasionally venture into the mountains, never to be heard from again. No one knew the true extent of the mountain range because no explorers or cartographers who had ventured into it had ever returned from their journeys.

The eerie, frightening mountain range did have one big advantage. It made it relatively easy to defend the kingdom. The Pumarians knew that no invaders would ever enter the kingdom from the north, east or west. This gave the Pumarians a feeling of security and complacency. Yes, it could be said that the entire Kingdom of Pumaria was very happy. The people took great pride in their various crafts and trades and worked very hard. Their reward was a peaceful, prosperous, harmonious existence in which people looked after each other. There were also frequent festivals and celebrations, a reflection of the genuine happiness of the people of Pumaria.

As the years went by, the export of apples and other products made the Kingdom of Pumaria a very wealthy land indeed. Everyone in the kingdom prospered, and a large number of the inhabitants lived either directly or indirectly from the cultivation of apples. King Giuseppe, because he was wise and benevolent, did not horde the profits. He shared his wealth with all the inhabitants of his kingdom.

It is easy to imagine that the apple, because of its economic importance, became almost sacred to the inhabitants of Pumaria. The most important festival held in the kingdom was the *sacra du pumu,* the festival of the apple, held in late autumn. It was held on the front lawn of the castle and featured many kinds of theatrical and musical performances and also many contests and tournaments. There was also a lot of eating, drinking, story-telling and general merriment. The sacra lasted for a whole week so that everyone in the kingdom would have an opportunity to attend for at least a couple of days.

Because Pumaria was so prosperous and so secure, and because it had such a wonderful climate, it was difficult for Giuseppe and his subjects to imagine that anyone or anything would ever be able to disturb their tranquility and happiness.

The castle of King Giuseppe and the royal family was located on the northern edge of the kingdom, not far from the foothills of the mountain range. This was considered to be the most secure place in the kingdom to build the residence of the royal family. The castle was located on the eastern bank of one of the rivers that flowed from the mountains to the sea. The castle had the shape of a perfect square and had a very large inner courtyard. In the very middle of the courtyard stood a large apple tree, and around the apple tree there were beautiful flower gardens. If viewed from the air, the castle would have looked like a large, elaborate square frame around a still life painting of flowers of red, white, yellow and violet.

King Giuseppe and his wife, Queen Filomena, had seven sons. The two eldest sons, Tosco and Doros, were excellent farmers and horticulturists. They were a great asset to their father's kingdom, because they were able to supervise most of the cultivation of apples and other fruits and vegetables grown in Pumaria. The third oldest son, Albano, was a very talented smith. He designed and fabricated many of the tools and implements that were used

in the kingdom.

The fourth son, Zoticus, was a carpenter and architect. He oversaw much of the construction and restoration work that was done on the castle and other buildings in the kingdom. The fifth son, Antonio, was a ship builder. His work was important for the exporting of apples and other goods from Pumaria. The sixth son, Stolos, was not only a good sailor but also a very gifted speaker and a clever merchant, so he was often asked by his father the king to travel to foreign lands in order to sell apples and other goods from Pumaria.

The seventh and youngest son, Laticus, was a jack of all trades, having learned a lot from each of his older brothers. This made him a very useful member of the family, since he was able to assist any of his older brothers in nearly all that they did. In spite of his young age, he was as strong as any of his older brothers.

Tosco, Doros and Albano were all married and had children. Zoticus, Antonio and Stolos were not married but had sweethearts whom they planned to marry someday. Laticus was the only son who was neither married nor betrothed.

Even though the Kingdom of Pumaria was well protected by the mountains and seemed immune to attack, King Giuseppe believed that the kingdom should be able to defend itself. For this reason, all young women and men in the kingdom, including the king's seven sons, were required to learn the skills needed for armed combat. All seven of Giuseppe's sons could handle a sword. Laticus, although he was the youngest of the seven, was acknowledged to be the best swordsman in the family. In fact, he was considered to be the finest swordsman in the entire kingdom. He was extremely quick and was very good at anticipating and countering the strategy of his opponent. He had never been defeated in a tournament. In one tournament event he even fended off seven opponents at once!

Laticus had a way of playing down his skills in handling a sword. "Our kingdom is so secure and so peaceful," he would say. "When will I ever need to use my sword except when competing in tournaments?"

Laticus, more than any other member of his family, was very fanciful and had a very active and vivid imagination. He had the habit of wandering around the northern border of the kingdom near the foothills of the mountain range during his spare time. Sometimes he even wandered into the foothills by himself. He was of course aware of the many frightening legends about the mountains, and of the explorers who had ventured into the mountains and never returned, so he never went any further than the foothills. Whenever Laticus returned to the castle after being in the foothills, he was scolded by his mother, Queen Filomena, for his foolhardiness. "You know you should not venture into those hills, Laticus!" she would cry. "Something terrible could happen to you. And besides, a prince should set a much better example for the rest of the people in the kingdom." King Giuseppe frequently added his own comments to the scolding remarks of his wife. "Laticus, my son, you know that you upset your mother terribly by going up into the hills. Please be more considerate." But Laticus could always find some way to dispel his parents' fears. "Anyway," Laticus would say, "I never go very far into the hills, and I never lose sight of the castle." This always seemed to appease his family, at least until the next time that he went for a walk in the foothills.

There was one time, however, that Laticus did in fact wander considerably farther than he ever had in the past. He left the castle at daybreak, before anyone else had risen, and headed for the foothills. He crossed completely over the foothills and went down into the valley on the other side. He then ascended the first row of mountains beyond the foothills and found himself looking down into a valley that he had never seen before. Beyond this valley were endless rows of even higher mountains. They looked very foreboding, like an endless army of giants. At first, Laticus was hesitant to descend into this unknown valley. He had heard too many stories. Unsure of what to do, Laticus turned around and took a few slow steps in the direction of his home, thinking that perhaps he should simply go back before he got into some kind of trouble. Before him were the familiar foothills, and behind them, in the far distance, a small speck on a field of green, was the castle of Pumaria. Somehow, the sight of his home gave Laticus courage. He turned back around and surveyed the valley again. "I see no sign of danger," he said to himself, "and it is still early in the day. I have plenty of time to explore this valley." And so, with one final look over his shoulder at the castle of Pumaria, Laticus started his descent into the unknown valley.

Laticus was now clearly no longer in the foothills, but in the mountains. He could no longer see the castle. He was in awe as he explored this newly discovered valley, and was very proud of himself for having ventured so far into this foreboding, unknown territory. As he looked around he realized that he was seeing plants and trees that he had never seen before. He was also hearing animal cries and birdcalls that were unfamiliar to him. He began to feel a bit uneasy, as though he did not belong there, but he continued to walk through the valley towards the next row of mountains.

After he had been exploring the valley for some time, Laticus began to feel the effects of the strenuous trek over the hills and into the mountains, and so he lay down on a patch of grass to take a rest. As he lay resting, his glance wandered up and down the sides of the mountains, and as he slowly scanned the rock formations on the side of one of the peaks his eyes landed on two adjacent caves that looked like a pair of cold, lifeless, cruel black eyes. As his glance continued downwards he could see a long, jagged slab of stone descending from between the two caves that resembled a nose. Below the nose was a horizontal row of jagged stones that resembled sharp teeth in a cruelly sneering mouth, and below the mouth was a patch of thick shrubbery that looked like a scraggly beard. It seemed that a huge, hideous face was staring down from the mountain and right at Laticus!

Laticus stared at this rocky visage with a sense of both horror and fascination. As his eyes continued to wander up and down the tall mountains, he realized that he could make out several other enormous, ugly faces. He counted seven faces in all. They seemed to be frozen in a cruel smile or a threatening scowl. Laticus suddenly felt extremely uneasy and began to feel that it was indeed very foolish to be in the mountains. He leaped up from his comfortable resting place and said aloud to himself, "There are seven ugly, giant faces scowling down at me from the sides of those mountains and I don't like it. I think it is time to leave." And so Laticus decided that he should turn around and go back home immediately, while the sun was still high. The thought of being in those mountains at night was unsettling even to someone as carefree and fearless as Laticus. Thus, the youngest prince of the Kingdom of Pumaria, with his sword at his side, started back through the valley and

towards the mountains to begin his journey home. The heat of the sun warmed his back as he traversed the valley.

After walking for a couple of hours, Laticus reached the edge of the valley and stood at the foot of one of the mountains. He was comforted and encouraged by the knowledge that when he reached the top of the mountain he would be able to see his castle in the distance, on the other side of the foothills. He began his ascent. Suddenly, the warmth of the sun vanished for an instant as a large shadow passed over Laticus and a breeze came out of nowhere, accompanied by a loud flapping sound. Laticus turned around instantly and looked straight up to see what it was that had cast such a shadow and caused such a draft of air. He found himself staring directly into the sun and was nearly blinded, but for a very brief moment he caught a glimpse of the silhouette of a very large bird, with a wingspan of at least twenty-five feet, flying around fifty feet in the air. The creature disappeared behind a precipice before Laticus could get a very good look at it. It all happened so fast that Laticus's first reaction was to think that he had hallucinated or that the sun had simply blinded him. But he could not believe for an instant that he had imagined the shadow that had blocked out the warmth of the sun, or the sudden draft of air, or the sound of flapping wings. "That bird was easily big enough to carry me away," Laticus said out loud and quickened his pace in order to return home as quickly as possible.

When Laticus finally reached home, just before dusk, he did not mention his adventure to anyone. When asked where he had been all day, he simply said that he had been visiting friends in a neighboring village. "If I told the truth," he reasoned with himself, "no one would believe my story anyway, and I would only be scolded again for venturing too far into the mountains." It was on that day that Laticus decided to discontinue his mountain wanderings, although he occasionally gazed at the hills from his room in the castle, watching in vain for anything that moved and thinking about the seven huge, ugly scowling faces that he had seen in the rock formations on the sides of the mountains and about the giant bird.

II. A thief in the night
'Nu latru i' notte
Un ladro nella notte

One autumn day after a very plentiful harvest, King Giuseppe decided to reward his seven sons for their great contributions to the success of his kingdom. He asked one of the most talented goldsmiths in the land to make seven apples of pure gold, each one the size of a normal Pumarian apple. Each apple was engraved with the name of one of the king's seven sons, Tosco, Doros, Albano, Zoticus, Antonio, Stolos and Laticus. It was decided that the seven golden apples would be attached to the branches of the large apple tree in the center of the inner court of the castle. Since it was autumn, the tree was bare except for the seven golden apples, which shone bright in the sunlight. During the summer months, when the tree bore fruit, the golden apples would blend in with the real apples in the tree, which were large and yellow and shone like gold in the bright sun. No one was worried that the apples would be stolen. The Kingdom of Pumaria was much too honest, peaceful and prosperous.

The year after the seven golden apples had been hung in the apple tree in the inner courtyard of the castle, there was another exceptionally good harvest and when Stolos set out on his annual voyage to sell apples and other goods to the various kingdoms across the sea, he asked Laticus to go with him. Laticus was always glad to go on a voyage, so the two of them left together. They planned to be gone for around two months. They would of course be home in time for the *sacra du pumu*.

Stolos and Laticus had been gone for around six weeks when something occurred that would badly shake the Kingdom of Pumaria. The morning started out like most autumn mornings. The members of the royal family, except for Stolos and Laticus, who were still on their journey, were in the refectory waiting to be served breakfast and chatting about how they planned to spend the beautiful autumn day that awaited them. The most important topic of conversation was the *sacra du pumu*, which would begin shortly after Stolos and Laticus had returned from their voyage. The servants were cheerfully serving fruit, bread, jam, milk, sausages, eggs and other delicious things, bantering with the royal family and playfully teasing them. Once everyone had been served, the royal family began to eat. During a lull in the conversation, Queen Filomena asked, "Was it my imagination, or was there a windstorm last night?" Zoticus said, "Come, mother! A windstorm at this time of year? You know that it doesn't get windy till early spring." King Giuseppe, who could never resist the opportunity to tease his wife, said, "You know your mother has an imagination that is so vivid that she sometimes doesn't know reality from fantasy!" But then Tosco spoke up. "Wait," he said. "I also heard wind during the night. I know that I didn't imagine it, because I was wide awake. The storm lasted only a few moments. It started out feint but very suddenly grew stronger. I could hear the rustling of the branches of the tree in the inner court. And then, as suddenly as the wind came, it was gone." Silence followed for several minutes. The Kingdom of Pumaria was so peaceful that any interruption in the tranquil routine of the Pumarians was unsettling. But soon the story of the unseasonal storm was

24

forgotten and the royal family returned to normal breakfast conversation.

Suddenly, one of the servant girls came bursting into the refectory, both hands covering her mouth, her eyes wide open, her skin pale. She ran up to the section of the table where the king and queen were sitting. As she let her hands drop from her mouth, tears began to stream from her eyes and she gasped, "One of the seven golden apples is missing!"

Immediately, all of the members of the family and all the servants ran down the stairs, out the door and into the inner courtyard to inspect the apple tree. They found themselves counting the golden apples over and over again, each time arriving at the same total: six! It was the apple of Tosco, the oldest son, that was missing. The ground around the tree was carefully searched, with no success. Albano climbed up the tree. "The apple probably fell and is stuck on one of the branches," he said. But after climbing all around the tree and scratching himself several times on the branches, Albano had to admit that the apple was gone.

During the time that Albano was in the tree searching for the missing apple, King Giuseppe's eyes were scanning the faces of all the family members and servants. He was a wise king who prided himself on his knowledge of people and his ability to read the face of a person like a book. He saw nothing but shock and sadness in the eyes of his family members and servants. He saw nothing suspicious, no guilt or nervousness. He did not expect to see anything suspicious in the eyes of anyone. Not only did he know all of his family very well, he also had a very personal relationship with all of the servants in the castle. The servants and cooks were all like members of the royal family. They were very well treated and well paid and their living quarters were very comfortable. King Giuseppe knew that none of his staff was capable of such a heinous act. He also knew that there were no grudges in his harmonious family and that no one had any motive for wanting to steal from Tosco or anyone else.

Albano climbed down from the tree, a look of great disappointment on his face. Everyone stared in disbelief at the place where the missing apple had hung. No one dared say a word. After a long silence the king spoke. "I know that this act of thievery was not committed by any member of my family or anyone else living in the castle. I also know that the castle is much too secure for anyone to have entered it by night. Something very uncanny and inexplicable has occurred. It will do us no good to stand here and stare at the apple tree. I suggest that we all go about our day's business and try not to think about what has happened. I will confer with my family and with advisers throughout the kingdom. If any of you have any thoughts or ideas, feel free to share them with me. In the meantime, let us go back inside the castle and try to finish breakfast, although I must say that I believe I have lost my appetite." Upon that, the royal family and the servants walked silently, slowly and dejectedly back into the castle.

Word of the theft spread quickly throughout the kingdom and left a feeling of shock and vulnerability everywhere. "The kingdom will never be the same," people were saying. No one could find the motivation to begin preparations for the *sacra du pumu*. When asked whether there should even be a sacra under the circumstances, King Giuseppe replied that he was not sure and wanted to think about it. "Before deciding whether or not to have a *sacra du pumu*," he said, "let us first see whether we can solve this mystery."

That night, after dinner, the king and his sons remained at the dinner table for a long time speculating about the disappearance of the golden apple. "What would anyone do with one of our golden apples?" said Tosco. "They are too famous. They could not be sold or even shown to anyone. No smith would melt them down for anyone. They are even engraved with our names." Antonio added, "No one has any reason to steal in our kingdom. No one is wanting in material things." "Not only that," said King Giuseppe. "Just consider the practical side of it. Who is going to break into our castle, enter our inner court and then climb that tree in the dead of night?" Queen Filomena entered the room at this moment. "Perhaps you are all wrong in assuming that the thief is human," she said. "Filomena," said King Giuseppe, "for once I cannot tease you about confusing reality and fantasy. This is a situation in which reality clearly overlaps with fantasy. Something has happened for which there is no natural explanation." "I think that the windstorm had something to do with it," said Queen Filomena. "But Mother," said her son Doros, "how can the wind steal an apple?" But King Giuseppe and his other sons tended to agree with the queen. A windstorm in autumn was too unusual to have been simply an innocent occurrence. It must have had something to do with the disappearance of the golden apple. "I am certain," the queen continued, "that whatever is responsible for this heinous act is from the mountainous region north of us. It is a frightening, evil place that can only produce wickedness." King Giuseppe spoke for everyone when he said, "The mountainous region is indeed the only possible source of evil in our good kingdom."

That night, as the reader can well imagine, no one in the entire kingdom slept very well. Members of the royal family and even the royal servants frequently walked to the window during the night to look out upon the inner court and the tree of the golden apples to watch for suspicious movements. For four nights the people of Pumaria were unsettled and could not sleep, and every morning there was an inspection of the tree to see if there were still six golden apples in it. After the fourth day, although the people of Pumaria were still feeling shocked, vulnerable, confused and sad, they were at least able to calm down and sleep through the night. Then, the impossible happened again.

III. Thieving wind

Vientu latru

Vento ladro

On the fifth night after the disappearance of the apple, Queen Filomena awoke suddenly and violently from her sleep and sat up quickly in bed. She saw that King Giuseppe slept calmly next to her. She was sure that she had heard a strange wind again. She heard someone run past her bedroom. She jumped out of bed, waking Giuseppe, ran to the door, threw it open, and stepped out of the room. By the light of the candles that lined the walls of the corridor, she could see her sons Tosco and Doros, one holding a torch, disappear down the stairway. "What is all this commotion?" cried Giuseppe. "I heard a windstorm again," answered Filomena. "Tosco and Doros must have heard it too, because they have gone downstairs to have a look."

Within a few moments everyone in the castle was awake and was following Tosco and Doros down the stairs and out the door into the inner courtyard. There, they could all see by torchlight that only five golden apples remained in the tree. Doros did not have to climb the tree to know that it was his apple that was gone. "This is an outrage!" he screamed. Everyone standing in the courtyard shared the same thoughts. There was clearly a connection between the wind and the theft of the apples. There seemed to be a super-natural force at work. The feeling of helplessness and vulnerability grew in the hearts of all present. It was also clear that there seemed to be a method to the thieving. It was the oldest brother who had lost his apple first, and then the second oldest. The third oldest brother, Albano, immediately started to think about how one might prevent the theft of any more apples, since his would probably be the next to be stolen. "I am going to start spending the night in that tree!" he said with angry determination. All attempts by the queen to dissuade her son from spending a night in the tree of the golden apples were thwarted.

Albano began to spend his nights in the tree. It was a very unpleasant experience. It was impossible to recline. Albano had to sit on a limb and lean against the trunk. The limb and trunk were of course hard and painful. The smaller branches were sharp and scratched the skin. Albano hardly slept at all during the night. He only dozed off for a few minutes at a time. At dawn, he came down from the tree very tired and with stiff, aching muscles throughout his entire body. In spite of his weariness, there was always work to do during the day, with no opportunity to catch up on sleep. By the sixth day Albano was truly exhausted. The whole family, particularly his wife and young daughter, were very concerned, but he insisted on spending yet another night in the tree, and he was much too proud to accept assistance or relief. Unfortunately, Albano was so tired that he fell into a deep sleep the instant that he took his place on the limb and leaned against the trunk. His slumber was so deep that not even the wind could wake him. It was the first ray of sunlight that finally roused him the next morning, and he awoke to see that there were only four golden apples hanging in the tree. And yes, it was the apple engraved with his name that had disappeared.

The disappearance of the third apple was very disheartening to the family of King Giuseppe. Zoticus, the fourth oldest son, was critical of his brother Albano. "How could you fall asleep like that?" he repeated over and over again. "Please don't talk to your brother like that," admonished Queen Filomena. "Albano was exhausted, and you know it." All of the brothers spoke defiantly. "We need to capture this thief and punish him severely," they all said. Queen Filomena was very concerned. "You talk of how you would punish this thief if you caught him," she said, "but you do not even know whom or what you are dealing with. If it is a supernatural being of some kind, you will be able to do nothing." The queen was afraid of provoking a being that seemed so powerful and mysterious and that could probably do great damage to the kingdom if it so desired. "Perhaps we should just let it have all seven golden apples, if that is what it will take to appease and get rid of it," she uttered in desperation. However, this remark met with great resistance from the king and his sons. Zoticus spoke up and said, "Mother, the thief must be stopped. If we allow him to simply take what he wants, he will end up plundering the entire Kingdom of Pumaria. I for one am not willing to surrender my apple, and I will be the next one to sit in the tree and wait." No one could disagree with Zoticus's remark.

Antonio, who was only a year younger than Zoticus, echoed his brother's words, saying, "I, too, am against the idea of just surrendering our golden apples. Stolos and Laticus are still away on their voyage, and I should perhaps not speak for them, but I cannot imagine that they would be willing to bow to this cowardly thief who sneaks into our kingdom by night and takes our prized possessions. However, perhaps the job of defending the remaining apples is too much for one man. Perhaps two or more of us should stand guard together." This suggestion was very badly received by Zoticus. "What?" he shouted. "Are you insinuating that this task is too much for me?" Zoticus was so insulted and became so irate that no one dared repeat Antonio's suggestion. Everyone felt that if Zoticus was going to be so adamantly insistent, it would be best to let him try to prove himself. King Giuseppe could of course have intervened, but he decided not to. He knew his seven sons, and he knew that even though they were very close and loved each other very much they were all extremely proud and extremely competitive, especially with each other. None of his sons

would ever accept help from one of his brothers. And so it was that King Giuseppe gave Zoticus his permission to stand guard alone.

The first night after the disappearance of Albano's golden apple, Zoticus planted himself in the tree. He made sure that he took a nap after dinner so that he would not fall asleep during the night. He did this for three consecutive nights, which remained uneventful. On the fourth night, at least four hours before sunrise, while Zoticus sat and waited, a sudden wind came up. Zoticus felt every muscle in his body go tense. With one hand he grasped one of the limbs above him to hold himself firmly in place. With the other hand, he drew his sword and held it ready for combat. The wind grew stronger. By the light of the moon Zoticus saw what looked like a low, small cloud whirling towards the tree. As he braced himself for the arrival of the cloud, a very sudden and powerful gust of wind seized Zoticus. He lost his grip of the limb and was blown from the tree. As he felt himself falling through the branches to the ground he dropped his sword in order to avoid falling on it and impaling himself. It all happened too fast for Zoticus to prepare himself for the fall. He landed on his shoulder and dashed his head against the ground, knocking himself unconscious. The people in the castle were awakened by the commotion and came running into the courtyard, only to find Zoticus half-conscious and groaning on the ground, and to find that yet another apple, the one belonging to Zoticus, was gone. Zoticus was badly injured. It appeared that his left arm was broken and his shoulder badly twisted.

The next night, Antonio felt obligated to climb the tree and defend the remaining three apples. He insisted that he would succeed where others had failed and, like his brothers before him, he refused to listen to any suggestions that it might behoove him to ask for assistance. Antonio decided to try something a bit different when he climbed up the tree. Instead of sitting close to the trunk as his brothers had done, he placed himself far out on one of the branches, almost within reach of the apple that was engraved with his name. "This way," he thought, "I will be closer to the edge of the tree and in a better position to strike at whatever it is that is stealing from us and humiliating the entire kingdom."

Albano watched as Antonio climbed the tree and took his place far out on a branch. He was feeling embarrassed that he had failed in his attempt to defend the apples, and he envied Antonio the opportunity that he now had to become a hero. "Antonio," he called up to his brother, "you have gone out too far on that branch. I do not believe that it will hold you. You should place yourself closer to the stem of the tree." "My dear older brother," Antonio replied from the tree, "with all due respect, you were unsuccessful in your attempt to protect our apples, and therefore I do not believe that you should be giving me advice. Could it be that you are just envious because I am up here and you are down there?" At this, Albano stomped angrily towards the entrance to the castle. But just before he passed through the castle entrance, he turned towards the tree. "Good luck, Antonio," he called to his younger brother. Antonio smiled at Albano and raised his sword in acknowledgement.

The sun set. The lights in the castle went out one by one as everyone retired. Silence reigned. It was a calm, clear night. As Antonio sat in the tree and waited, he had to admit to himself that his brother Albano might very well have been right. The branch under him felt not only uncomfortable but weak. Nonetheless, he decided to adhere to his plan and to

position himself as close to the edge of the tree as possible.

As fate would have it, on Antonio's very first night in the tree, the wind came up again. Antonio drew his sword, watched and waited. "How odd," he thought, as he looked up at the moonlit sky, "that there would be a storm on such a clear night." Suddenly, Antonio could see a dark object, at least twenty feet high, moving towards him in a whirling motion. He held his sword far behind him and was ready to strike, but before he even had time to react he felt the branch beneath him give way and snap. Antonio instinctively let his sword drop and reached out to grasp another branch. The words of warning of his brother Albano echoed in his ears as this branch also broke and Antonio crashed through several other branches and landed on the ground. He was disoriented and barely conscious. The noise woke up several people in the castle and some of them ran to Antonio's aid, but by the time they reached the courtyard, the windstorm was gone and the apple engraved with Antonio's name had disappeared, leaving only two golden apples in the tree. Antonio had unfortunately fallen from the tree just before the theft took place and thus he had not seen what really happened. He felt great shame and embarrassment at his failure.

The next morning the king and queen and their sons discussed what should be done. Tosco, the oldest son, said, "There are only two apples left. I think we should remove them from the tree and hide them in the castle." Queen Filomena categorically rejected this suggestion. "If we do that," she said, "the thief will enter the castle and ransack it if necessary in order to find the apples that he seems to be obsessed with. No, I must insist that the apples remain where they are, come what may." No one could offer an argument against Queen Filomena's statement, and so the apples were left in the tree. Despair was settling like a dark cloud on the Kingdom of Pumaria. No one knew what to do. "Sometimes I think that this is all my fault," the queen confided in her husband. "Why ever would you think such a ridiculous thing?" Giuseppe replied to her. "Because," she said, "just before this catastrophe began, I was thinking that our land was so secure, so prosperous, so contented, that it was invincible. I see now that it is dangerous to be too complacent." Giuseppe comforted her. "Don't be superstitious, My Queen. Your complacent thoughts had nothing to do with this. We cannot comprehend what is going on, but blaming ourselves will get us nowhere." Giuseppe tried to conceal his concerns about the future of his kingdom. He knew that it had been weakened by the recent events, and he was concerned that things would only grow worse. He could not help but think of how shocked and disappointed his two youngest sons would be when they returned to Pumaria from their voyage.

IV. Stolos and Laticus return
Tornunu Stolos e Laticus
Il ritorno di Stolos e Laticus

The morning after the loss of Antonio's apple, at the main harbor of the Kingdom of Pumaria, far away from the castle, a ship arrived. Stolos and Laticus were returning from a very successful voyage. They had contracted business with three other kingdoms and they were very cheerful. The two brothers bade farewell to the crew of their vessel and began their short walk down the pier to the inn where they had left their horses. They were planning to freshen up there, to dine, to rest for a couple of hours, and then begin the long ride home to the castle. They smiled at the people they saw in the port and greeted them heartily, but they were surprised that their cheerfulness was answered by despondency. Everyone in the port seemed sluggish and depressed. No one smiled. It was not normal for the Kingdom of Pumaria. Stolos turned to Laticus and asked, "Are we in the right kingdom? It looks like Pumaria, but it could not be!"

When they entered the inn and found that even the usually joyful innkeeper seemed depressed, the two brothers had had enough. They asked the innkeeper to tell them what was wrong. He of course obeyed the request of the two princes and told them everything, including the fact that the *sacra du pumu*, even though it had not been officially canceled, was for the moment being postponed pending a solution to the great mystery of the theft of the golden apples. Stolos and Laticus could not believe their ears. They decided to dispense with freshening up, dining and relaxing, and instead immediately began their ride to the castle.

Just before sunset, when Stolos and Laticus arrived at the castle, they were spotted by one of the servants who had been watching for their return, and everyone descended to meet them. What should have been a joyful reunion with talk of a successful voyage and the approaching *sacra du pumu* was instead a sad conversation about the mysterious attack on the kingdom. After hearing all the details, Stolos announced that he would spend the night in the tree. "I will not make the same mistakes that my older brothers have made," he vowed.

Stolos did in fact start spending the night in the tree of the golden apples. Six nights went by uneventfully. On the seventh night, while Stolos waited, sword in hand, the sky suddenly clouded up, blotting out the moon and stars, and it grew very dark. It became so dark that he could not see his hand in front of his face. Stolos had counted on the light of the moon to help him keep watch, but because of the cloud cover, there was not even a bit of starlight to help him see. "I should descend the tree and light a torch," he said out loud to himself. But just as he was about to climb down, the wind came up suddenly. The gusts of wind became very strong. Stolos was nearly swept out of the tree, but he held on. He could hear a whirling sound as the windstorm got closer and closer. After a very short time, Stolos was certain that the whirlwind was right next to the tree, but he could see nothing because of the darkness. He lashed with his sword in the direction of the two remaining golden apples, but he could not see what he was striking at. Then, as suddenly as the wind

had appeared, it was gone. In the dead calm of the night, Stolos slowly and carefully climbed down the tree and stumbled through the dark into the castle, where he found a torch, lit it and returned to the courtyard to confirm what he had feared: The golden apple bearing his name was gone.

V. The thief finishes his business
U latru finisce l'opera
Il ladro completa l'opera

The next morning, Laticus vowed to resolve the problem once and for all. "If this mysterious thief succeeds in getting the last apple, which is my apple," he cried, "who knows what he will come after next?" Laticus began to plan his strategy. He carefully analyzed how the other apples had been lost, and the errors that his older brothers had made. Albano had fallen asleep. Zoticus had been knocked from the tree by the wind. Antonio, who had wanted to be as close to the apples as possible, had placed himself too far from the trunk of the tree and had sat on a branch that could not hold him. Stolos was blinded by the darkness and could do nothing. Laticus knew that he would have to make sure to prevent all of those things from happening to him.

The very next night, Laticus carried out his strategy. First, he built a fire so that he would be able to see even if the sky became cloudy. He built it fifty paces from the tree. "If the fire is too close to the tree," he reasoned, "the wind might extinguish it as it rushes by." The firewood that he used was very dry, and he coated it with a special oil that would cause it to burn through the night. He built a small stone wall in front of the fire to provide more protection against the wind. He then climbed the tree. He moved his golden apple, the only one remaining in the tree, to a branch that was a sword's length from the trunk of the tree. He then placed himself immediately next to the trunk, where the branches were thick and could easily support his weight. With a strong leather strap that he had tied around his waist, he fastened himself tightly to the trunk. No gust of wind would be able to blow him from the tree. And since his apple was now only a sword's length from him, he would easily be able to defend it. In order to make sure that he did not fall asleep, he had not only a sword but also a dagger in the tree with him. Whenever he felt himself dozing off, he placed the dagger between his knees with the blade directly under his chin. If he nodded, the dagger pricked his chin and woke him up.

Laticus repeated this ritual every night for seven nights without incident. Then, on the eighth night, it happened. The wind came up. It grew louder. Laticus focused his vision in the direction that the wind was coming from. Suddenly, he could see a whirlwind come over the castle wall. It was heading straight for the tree in which he was sitting. The fire that he had built began to flicker but did not go out. It was far enough from the tree to be safe from the wind but close enough to provide adequate light to Laticus. The closer the whirlwind got to the tree, the stronger the gusts of wind became, but the leather strap held Laticus firmly in place. As the whirlwind drew nearer and nearer, Laticus could see that it was around twenty-five feet high and that it looked like an opaque, rapidly spinning cloud. Its rotating motion was faster than anything that Laticus had ever witnessed, and it seemed to have a dizzying effect. When the whirlwind reached the tree and the branch to which the sole remaining golden apple was attached, it continued its rapid, spinning motion, but came to rest. Laticus held his sword over his head, ready to strike. Suddenly, a huge hand

covered with black hair came out of the whirlwind in a flash, quickly grasped the golden apple and started to move back into the whirlwind. But just before the hand could disappear back into the windy cloud, Laticus wielded his sword masterfully, and the sword found its mark. Blood spewed forth from the wound that Laticus had inflicted upon the huge hand. Unfortunately, the blow that Laticus had landed was not enough to stop the theft of his apple, and the huge, bleeding hand disappeared back into the whirlwind, tightly holding its prize of gold. In an instant the whirlwind darted away from the tree and disappeared over the castle wall.

VI. The search begins

Vanu a circari

La ricerca

The next morning, the king and his sons stood beneath the tree that had once housed the seven golden apples. Laticus told the story of what had happened the night before. "How can you be sure that you actually struck the hand?" asked King Giuseppe. "Very simple," Laticus replied, as he pointed to several large drops of blood on the grass below the branch where the apple had hung.

Laticus started to walk slowly in the direction in which the whirlwind had disappeared, his eyes focused on the ground. "Look!" he cried with excitement. "Here are more drops of blood!" The king immediately ordered all of his sons, except for Zoticus, who had still not recovered from his fall, to arm themselves and join together to help follow the trail of blood. The search went on for hours and led the party into the foothills to the north of the kingdom, to places where Laticus had never ventured. Sometimes the party would lose the trail, but someone was always able to find drops of blood on the ground, or on vegetation, or on rocks. The trail of blood led the party through the foothills and up the side of a mountain. All the members of the search party felt extremely uneasy about entering the infamous mountain range.

When the party reached the top of the mountain, the trail of blood led them to a large hole in the ground. It seemed to be a kind of cave or tunnel that was about fifteen feet in diameter and seemed to go straight down. The drops of blood on the edge of the hole indicated that the wounded thief had indeed descended into it. Because the cave went straight downward and there were no steps or ladders, it was hard to imagine how anyone could have entered it. Stones were thrown into the hole, but no sound of their landing was heard. "The hole must be very deep," said the king. "The only way to continue this pursuit will be to lower someone on a rope. We shall therefore return home now and tomorrow morning we will begin to manufacture the longest rope ever made. We shall bind together all the ropes in the kingdom if necessary, until we have a rope that will extend to the bottom of this hole. And then we shall return here and continue to pursue this thief who has threatened our kingdom." The party then made its way back down the mountain and returned to the castle.

The next day, all the craftsmen and craftswomen in Pumaria who knew how to make rope were asked to weave a strong rope that could hold a grown man and withstand the elements. This work continued for three days and the result was more than a hundred ropes, which were then spliced together to form one very long rope. A large, wooden spool with wide rims was also constructed and mounted on a sturdy four-wheeled cart. The spool was equipped with a large crank so that it could be turned. One end of the rope was firmly attached to the inside of the spool, immediately adjacent to one of the rims, and the rope was then wound around the spool by turning the crank. While one man turned the crank two others guided the rope so that it would be evenly wound around the spool. Once the rope had been completely wound up, the very end of it was split in two and the two ends were

attached to a flat wooden board so as to form a seat for whomever would be lowered into the hole.

The next morning, as soon as the first ray of sunlight could be perceived, the king and all of his sons except the injured Zoticus set out to return to the mysterious cave. The cart that held the large spool was pulled along by a team of six horses. Two other horses carrying food, water and supplies also accompanied the party. The king also brought along a large cowbell. Although the mountain was high, it was not very steep and the path to the top was not very rocky. It was thus possible for the horses to pull the spool to the site of the hole without too much difficulty.

There was of course a heated discussion about who should be lowered into the hole. The king decided to follow the normal practice among royalty and leave first choice to the eldest son. Tosco said that he would like to be the one to avenge the family. He slung a bag of food and a canteen of water over his shoulder, strapped his sword to his side, and took his place on the seat at the end of the rope, which was hanging a few feet into the hole. Doros, who was chosen to operate the crank, then began to lower Tosco into the hole. Just as Tosco started his descent the king gave him the cowbell and said, "In case you change your mind and want to return to the surface, just ring the bell and we will reel you back up." So, Tosco took the bell with him. He looked confident and brave as he bade farewell to his father and brothers.

The feeling of being lowered into an unknown hole was eerie indeed. When Tosco looked up he could see the entrance to the hole grow smaller and smaller as he was lowered deeper and deeper. When he looked down he saw nothing but blackness, with no indication of an end to the tunnel. He sometimes thought he heard strange noises and smelled strange odors. He began to sense the presence of inhuman, evil things. He did not know whether he was imagining things or not. He began to think of his wife and children, who might never see him again. He began to perspire. That is when he realized that he was beginning to panic. He took the cowbell and shook it frantically.

Within seconds he felt the great relief of being pulled upward. This did not cause his fear to dissipate, however. The darkness was so frightening that he did not experience true relief until both of his feet were out of the hole and touching the ground. He was immediately flooded with questions from everyone about what it had been like. Everyone listened with fascination and terror as Tosco described his descent. "I was not only afraid for myself," he said, "but also for my wife and children, who I feared might never see me again." Upon hearing this, King Giuseppe declared that he would not allow anyone to descend into the hole who had children. "It would be most unfair," he explained. "I therefore refuse to allow Doros and Albano to descend. Zoticus is not here because he is injured. This means that it is up to Antonio, Stolos and Laticus to decide. I will allow the oldest to decide first. Antonio, will you enter the cave and avenge our kingdom?"

After hearing Tosco's tale, Antonio was none too anxious to enter the hole, but he felt obligated to try. He had not been inside the cave for long when he started to feel threatened by unseen things and rang the bell. It was now Stolos's turn. Stolos was not cowardly. On the contrary, he was considered to be bold. Stolos did in fact venture further down than his

predecessors. Nonetheless, after a certain point, he was also overcome by fear because he sensed a presence in the darkness but could see absolutely nothing. He began to hallucinate and to panic, and when he felt that he might faint he began to ring the bell furiously. Stolos was quickly pulled back to the surface. It was now up to the youngest son, Laticus.

While his older brothers were being lowered into the cave, Laticus had been watching the spool and concluded that the rope was probably not long enough. He went to his father and said, "Father, we need to double the length of the rope. There was not very much left on the spool when Stolos rang the bell." The king then said, "Let us leave the spool and rope here and return to the castle. We shall then again enlist the assistance of everyone in the kingdom with experience in rope-weaving."

Within four days, hundreds of additional ropes had been woven. At sunrise on the fifth day, the ropes were loaded on a team of packhorses and another journey to the hole was made by the king, six of his sons and several rope weavers. Once the party arrived at the hole, all the ropes were unloaded and spliced together into one extremely long one. The splicing lasted the entire day. King Giuseppe remarked, "I believe that this new rope is long enough to reach all the way to the castle and back. When we splice it to the rope that is already on the spool, perhaps we will have a rope that is long enough to reach the bottom of the cave. But let us now return to the castle so that we will be there before sunset. We will come back here tomorrow morning early and resume our work."

The next morning at daybreak the king and his six sons returned to the hole. They were accompanied by some of the men and women who worked in the castle and who wanted to see Laticus off on his mission. Before Laticus could be lowered into the hole, there was work to be done. First, the sitting board was removed from the rope that was wound around the spool. The tip of the new rope was then spliced to the rope on the spool as a very long extension. The extension then had to be reeled up. All the men, including the king, took turns turning the crank while two others guided the rope evenly onto the spool. After several hours, when all the rope had been reeled up, the spool was completely full. The diameter of the wound rope equaled that of the very large rims of the spool. The wooden seat was reattached and the rope was lowered just inside the hole. The search could now continue. All the members of the party grew silent and all eyes were on Laticus. Everyone was filled with a sense of fear but also of hope. Everyone had faith in Laticus.

Laticus put on the belt that held his sheathed sword and dagger. His brother Tosco handed him a sack packed with food and a canteen full of water, which he hung over his shoulder. He then unceremoniously sat down on the sitting board at the end of the rope and held on to the rope with both hands. His father brought him the cowbell, but he refused it. "No, Father, I will not take the cowbell with me on my descent, for I am not coming back without the seven golden apples." With that, Laticus was lowered into the hole and vanished into the darkness.

VII. The descent

'A scisa

La discesa

The descent into the hole was slow and frightening. The sound of the spool turning became more and more feint, and the circle of light from the surface became smaller and smaller. Laticus's mind was racing as he tried to imagine what fate awaited him. He also began to wonder if the thief who had stolen the golden apples would perhaps return to Pumaria to steal other things or to harm the people there while he was on this bold mission. In that case, what good did it do for him to be descending into a deep tunnel that may lead to nothing but his death?

After being lost in thought for some time Laticus realized that something was missing. It was the sound of the turning of the spool, which had now become completely inaudible. He looked upwards and realized that he could also no longer see the light from the surface. The darkness was now complete. Like his brothers before him, he began to imagine that he was hearing strange sounds and smelling strange odors. He began to hallucinate, seeing strange images in the darkness. "Not taking that bell with me was perhaps the biggest mistake I have ever made," he said out loud, "although if I rang it now they would never hear it anyway." He began to hope that the rope was not long enough to reach the bottom. "If the rope is completely used up," he thought, "maybe the people on the surface will simply reel me back up." But he knew that this would merely delay the process, because if he were pulled back to the top, within a few days the rope weavers would lengthen the rope even more.

As time passed and the descent continued, Laticus found himself overcoming his fear. He simply became more and more determined to reach his destination and avenge the theft of the seven golden apples. His only fear was of hunger and thirst, because he had consumed all of the provisions that he had brought with him. Suddenly, Laticus felt a surge of excitement and exhilaration when he thought that he saw a dim point of light appear far below him. "Am I hallucinating," he asked himself, "or does this tunnel really have an end?" As he went lower and lower and the point of light grew larger, he knew that he was not imagining it. He was about to arrive in a place where no one from his kingdom had ever been before.

When Laticus finally reached the bottom of the hole he found himself in a dimly lit chamber. Although the light was weak, it took a few moments for his eyes to adjust to it after having been in darkness for so long. He saw that the illumination of the chamber came from two torches on the wall. Near the torches was a huge iron door at least twenty feet high with no handle or latch. Around six feet in front of the door stood the bronze statue of a giant warrior. The warrior wore a helm and a breast plate and held a large sword in his right hand. There was a sign at the foot of the statue that read, "Whosoever is strong enough to pull the sword from my hand will pass through the iron door."

Laticus dropped the empty sack and canteen that had contained his provisions of

food and water, laid down his sword and dagger, and began to consider how he might re-move the sword from the hand of the statue. He realized that he would have to mount the statue and pull the sword upwards in order to extract it from the warrior's hand.   He put both of his hands around the left hand of the bronze warrior and pulled himself up. He then wrapped his legs around the statue's waist in order to hold himself in place. He could not put his hands around the blade of the sword because it was too sharp. He could not put his hands around the hilt because it was covered by the bronze hand of the warrior. He took hold of the guard of the sword with one hand and with the other hand he grabbed the pom-mel. He then began to pull the sword towards him. He pulled and pulled and his muscles grew more and more tense. When he felt the sword begin to loosen slightly, he pulled even harder, until the sword finally came loose from the warrior's hand and dropped to the floor. Suddenly, the great iron door began to creak open. As the door slowly opened, the light of day began to enter the chamber, and when the door was finally wide open, the room was flooded with sunlight.

Laticus leapt down from the statue and ran to the iron door. He was astonished to see that it opened directly onto a dirt path that led into a dense forest. In order to see better, Laticus climbed a very tall tree on the side of the dirt path. When he reached the top he could see that the forest extended far in all directions, and that it was in a valley surrounded on all sides by tall, intimidating mountains. The sun had just risen above the mountains and it was early morning. Laticus then realized that his descent into the cave had lasted through the entire night.

Looking in the direction that the dirt path seemed to come from, Laticus could see in the far, far distance a hilly area at the edge of the mountains, and in the hills he could vaguely make out what seemed to be a castle on a hilltop overlooking a town or village. "I wonder where I am," Laticus said to himself. "The long tunnel that I have descended seems to have led to another valley deep inside the mountain range that surrounds my kingdom. This dirt path below me must surely lead to that distant castle. I must go there, for that is where the seven golden apples must be." Laticus climbed down the tree and reentered the chamber from which he had just exited to retrieve his sword and dagger. He noticed that the rope that had borne him through the tunnel was no longer being lowered. It had been completely unraveled! Laticus realized this and knew that he had been very fortunate be-cause the rope had been just long enough for his descent.

Laticus walked out of the chamber. All he could think about was his mission to find the seven golden apples. And so, tired, thirsty and hungry, his sword and dagger at his sides, Laticus walked down the dirt path and disappeared into the forest.

VIII. Entry into a new world

Trasuta 'intra n'atru munnu

Ingresso in un nuovo mondo

As he walked through the forest, Laticus would sometimes catch sight of wild animals. They looked dangerous at first, resembling lions, wolves, bears and wild boars. Laticus drew his sword in case he might have to defend himself. However, the animals revealed themselves to be anything but dangerous. As soon as Laticus came near them they quickly ran behind a tree or into the undergrowth, where they cowered and tried to remain out of sight. Laticus could not understand why animals that would normally be ferocious and dangerous would act so cowardly. A few times, Laticus stopped in his tracks and stared at the animals that he saw huddled behind trees and plants. The more he observed these extremely timid animals, the more he realized that there was something very eerie about them, because their faces had almost human features. Laticus resheathed his sword. He felt no threat from these strange, pitiful creatures.

After walking for some time and entering deeper and deeper into the forest, Laticus came to a small clearing. There he met an old man seated on a bench on the side of the path. Next to the bench was a cauldron over a smoldering fire. From the cauldron came the appetizing aroma of vegetable stew. On the ground behind the old man's bench there lay several wooden bowls and spoons and three waterskins that bulged with liquid. Laticus was very excited about meeting an inhabitant of this strange place, and hoped that this old man would be able to help him. "Good day, sir," Laticus said to him. "I am Prince Laticus of Pumaria. Can you tell me where I am? I am a stranger here." "I am Eliades," answered the old man. "You are in the Valley of the Giant with Seven Heads. Pray tell, young man, what is it that brings you to such a dangerous place?" Laticus said, "Before I answer your question, I wonder if you could spare me some food and drink. My supplies ran out hours ago and I am growing weak from lack of nourishment." Eliades gave Laticus one of the three waterskins and said, "Drink." The cool water was very soothing to his parched throat. Using a spoon, the old man filled one of the wooden bowls with stew from the cauldron and handed the bowl and spoon to Laticus. Laticus quickly ate the stew and the old man, seeing that Laticus was still hungry, gave him a second helping.

Feeling well fed and refreshed, Laticus sat down on the bench next to Eliades and proceeded to tell him all about Pumaria and the events that had led him to this forest. "I have come to retrieve our golden apples," Laticus said forcefully. The old man then told Laticus all about the valley. He explained that the valley had once been a peaceful, prosperous land ruled by a benevolent queen named Fausta, but that nearly two years ago the Giant with Seven Heads had driven the queen and her daughter, Princess Lina, from their castle and was now occupying the castle himself. The giant was terrorizing the valley. He had killed many people arbitrarily and had forced many others into slavery. Eliades had himself lost a son to the cruel giant. The inhabitants of the valley, even the royal family, were forced to hide out in cellars or even in caves. No one had ever defeated the giant because he was

large, hideous and strong and had magical powers. "Tell me, Eliades," said Laticus, "if I am successful in retrieving the seven golden apples, do you think that I will ever make it back to my home?" The old man answered, "We can talk about that when the time comes, that is, if you are successful in your mission and are not killed by the Giant with Seven Heads."

Laticus was full of questions for the old man, who told him everything he could about the queendom. He then advised Laticus that he should probably be on his way because he still had a long way to go in order to reach the castle. "I would like to ask one last question before I go," said Laticus. "Who are those pitiful, timid creatures in the forest, those animals with human-like faces?" Eliades explained that those creatures had once been normal people but that the Giant with Seven Heads had put them under a spell because they had cursed him. He could have simply killed them outright, but in order to demonstrate his terrifying magical powers he put them under a curse instead. "I am the caretaker of those animals," said Eliades. "I give them food and drink." Laticus became very concerned. "Is there any way to prevent the giant from turning me into one of those miserable animals?" he asked. Eliades replied, "The giant's curse will only work if you let fear into your heart. If you banish fear, the giant's curse is powerless." With that, Laticus thanked Eliades, bade him farewell, and continued on his journey.

In the early afternoon, Laticus reached the end of the forest, where he found a village at the foot of a small mountain. On the top of the mountain there stood a beautiful castle. Laticus knew that he had arrived at the place that he had seen from the tree just after arriving in the Valley of the Giant with Seven Heads. There was absolutely no sign of life in the village, not even the barking of a dog or the mewing of a cat. Laticus walked up the hill to the castle. A gardener was working on the castle grounds. Laticus approached him. The man seemed very surprised. "What is this look of astonishment?" Laticus asked with a jocular tone in his voice. The gardener answered, "You are obviously not from around here. No one who is from around here would ever come near this place. This is the castle of the Giant with Seven Heads. It used to be….." "I know all about it," Laticus interrupted him. "And it is precisely this place that I was seeking." Laticus then told him the whole story of the loss of the seven golden apples and of his plans to retrieve them even if it meant fighting the Giant with Seven Heads. He told him that he would be very grateful for any help and advice that he could give him. "Young man," said the gardener, "the giant has killed so many young men like you. I shudder to think of the fate that awaits you if you insist on battling him." The gardener then told Laticus his own story.

The gardener, whose name was Fossor, had been a caretaker for Queen Fausta before the giant came, subdued the land and forced the queen and her daughter to flee. Now, he was forced to work for the giant. The giant kept his family imprisoned in the castle. If he tried to do anything to hurt the giant, or if he tried to escape, the giant would kill his wife and children. The gardener did, however, describe for Laticus the interior of the castle and explain the way in which the rooms were laid out and connected. He also gave Laticus some very useful advice. "It is early afternoon," he said, "and this is probably the best time to attack the giant. He will have just taken his midday meal, so he will be oversated and inebriated, and he may even be napping. It would be best to surprise him while he sleeps. I must warn you again, however, that many brave young men have attempted to fight the giant, and

all have been brutally killed."

      Laticus was not intimidated by Fossor's words. On the contrary, he was emboldened by them, and even though he knew that he should be feeling exhausted after all that he had been through, he was nonetheless feeling excited and anxious to continue on his mission. He decided that this would be the best time to avenge the actions of the Giant with Seven Heads. He thanked the gardener for all the information and advice and made his way towards the castle.

IX. Duel
'A litica
Duello

Laticus entered the castle through a side door that the gardener had told him about. He found himself in the cellar. As he walked down a narrow passageway he passed by a dungeon secured by an enormous metal lock and full of around twenty very forlorn looking people. They looked underfed and were as quiet as a mouse. "Who are you?" asked Laticus, but he was immediately chastised by one of the prisoners, who loudly whispered, "Please don't talk. If the giant hears us make a sound he will become very angry and kill us." He then explained to Laticus in a soft whisper that he and his fellow prisoners were the slaves of the giant. The giant let them out once a day and then forced them to do hard labor in the castle. Anyone who had ever tried to escape had been easily captured by the giant and squashed like a bug. They were given very little to eat. The giant always kept the keys to the dungeon on his belt so that no one would dare try to take them. Laticus explained to the prisoners that the giant had stolen seven golden apples from his kingdom and that he, Prince Laticus of Pumaria, had come to retrieve them. The prisoners expressed their deep regret that such a nice, brave young prince like Laticus was about to meet a horrible fate.

Laticus continued past the dungeon and down the passageway until he came to a stairway. He walked up the stairs and found a door that opened into a large foyer at the main entrance to the castle. He saw a staircase that led upstairs, but decided to first explore the main floor. He moved silently through the entire main floor but found all the rooms empty. He then returned to the foyer near the main entrance and with his sword drawn began to move slowly and quietly up the stairs. As he neared the top he began to perceive the sound of snoring. He let his ears lead him towards the source of the snoring, which grew louder and more thunderous the closer Laticus got to it. Finally, Laticus came to the room where the sound was coming from. He peeked inside and to his horror saw an enormous, hideous, seven-headed giant slumped over a huge table. He had laid all seven of his large, ugly heads on the table, and they were all loudly snoring at once. "No wonder he snores so loud," thought Laticus. On the table Laticus could see large articles of cutlery and crockery and a large wine bottle that appeared to be empty. There were several large wooden crates on the floor that the servants had apparently used for carrying the giant's food up into the dining room. And there, on a high mantelpiece over a burning hearth, were the seven golden apples! It was with great satisfaction that Laticus noticed the large cut on the left hand of the giant. "That will be the least of the wounds that I will have inflicted upon you, you cowardly monster," Laticus thought.

But as Laticus beheld his huge adversary, he began to feel desperate. "How can I possibly defeat such a rival?" he asked himself. "I hope that the empty wine bottle means that he will be drunk and easier to out-maneuver." With no further thought he decided that the best thing to do would be to attack immediately, before the giant woke up, and to try to cut off as many heads as possible before the giant could get up from the table. The table and the

chairs around it were quite high. Laticus quietly moved one of the wooden crates next to the table, stood on it, jumped up and grabbed the edge of a chair. He then pulled himself up onto the chair. He did this very quietly, but the snoring of the giant was so loud that it was hard to imagine that anything could be heard over it. Once he was on the chair, Laticus jumped up and grabbed the edge of the table and pulled himself up. He was now standing on the table and staring at seven huge, hairy, ugly, snoring heads. It was then that he remembered the rock formations in the mysterious valley that resembled seven hideous faces.

Laticus walked slowly across the table to where the snoring heads were resting, raised his sword over his head, calculated his move, and lowered three savage blows within the twinkling of an eye. He had severed three of the giant's heads. The giant immediately woke up from his sleep and leapt up with a roar of savage rage. Laticus could see that the giant was at least twenty feet tall and even more horrifying when he was standing. His black eyes were cold and lifeless and the hair on his heads was scraggly and disheveled, as were the beards beneath his cruel, sneering mouths.

The blows that Laticus had landed were so powerful that the three severed heads had flown off the table and onto the floor. To Laticus's horror, however, the heads rolled around on the floor for a few moments and then flew through the air and landed right back where they had been, on the giant's shoulders! At this, Laticus gasped and felt his legs go weak. "I cannot combat magical powers like this," he thought, but he remembered the words of Eliades. "I cannot be afraid," he said to himself.

When the giant saw Laticus he lunged at him, but he was in fact a bit sluggish because of the wine and because of being suddenly awakened from a deep sleep. Laticus was able to step out of the way and the giant landed with all his weight on the table. Laticus seized this opportunity to wield his sword again and was able to chop off two of the giant's heads. However, once again, the heads rolled around on the floor for a few moments and then flew back onto the body of the giant as though they had never been severed. "You've got to keep those heads from flying back onto his body," Laticus admonished himself.

The giant lifted himself up off the table and again lunged at Laticus. Once again, Laticus was able to dodge the giant, whose upper torso went sliding past Laticus on the table top, and once again Laticus was able to land a blow and sever a head. This time, however, Laticus leaped off the table onto the chair, jumped down onto the floor, snatched up the rolling head, and put it into one of the wooden crates. He slammed the lid of the crate shut and jumped up on top of it. He could feel the crate bouncing up and down beneath his feet, but the head was unable to free itself and could not return to the body of the giant. Laticus suddenly felt a surge of hope and confidence. He now knew that there was a way to defeat this monster!

The giant stood up and Laticus could see that he was going to try to get the crate and retrieve his head. Laticus remained on top of the crate and waited for the giant to come towards him. The giant knew by now that the sword of Laticus was something to be reckoned with. He made several stabbing motions with his hands as though he were trying to grab Laticus but he had to keep pulling his hands back as Laticus swung his sword. On one of his attempts to bend down and grab Laticus, the giant got too close and Laticus took advantage

of the opportunity and chopped off another head. While the giant screamed in angry pain and reeled backwards Laticus immediately jumped on the rolling head and secured it in another crate to keep it from rejoining the giant's body. He now stood with one foot on each of the two crates, each containing a head. Laticus could see that the giant had been weakened by the loss of two heads and was becoming disoriented.

Once again the giant made an attempt to grab Laticus and got too close, and once again Laticus`s sword whistled as it cut through the air and sent another one of the giant's heads flying. In a heartbeat Laticus jumped onto this head and reached for another crate in order to secure it. The giant saw this as an opportunity to go for the other two crates in order to get his heads back. However, when he bent down to pick up a crate, Laticus was there and his sword was too fast for the giant. Laticus was able to lop off two heads this time, which sent the giant reeling again. This gave Laticus plenty of time to secure both of the heads in a crate. The crates bounced up and down as the heads attempted to exit them and return to the shoulders of the giant. Laticus was afraid that the heads would escape because he could not stand on so many crates at once, but fortunately the crates were firmly sealed and the heads remained trapped inside.

At this, the giant retreated into a corner. He was now staggering badly and blood was streaming from the places where five heads had been. He suddenly began to spin around, faster and faster, until he turned into a whirlwind, and started to move towards Laticus, who was guarding the five crates that held the giant's heads. At first Laticus was intimidated by the giant's metamorphosis, but he quickly regained his confidence and stood ready as the whirlwind approached. "The last time you came at me like that I nearly cut off your hand," Laticus cried aloud. "What will it be this time?"

As the whirlwind moved slowly towards him, Laticus quickly stacked the five crates on top of each other and climbed onto the top of the stack. He suddenly began to feel feint. He had been fighting for some time and was beginning to feel the effects. He thought of his family in Pumaria and, miraculously, was able to muster up a second wind. When the whirlwind got to within a few feet of Laticus, he began to rotate his sword in a circular motion over his head as fast as he could move it. His strength started to fail him again and the circular motion of his sword was making him dizzy. The whirlwind started to move backwards slightly, seemingly intimidated by the swirling sword, and at this Laticus simply sliced into the whirlwind itself, hoping to hit the giant. He again heard the giant roar with pain as a head came flying out of the whirlwind. Laticus jumped on the head and quickly secured it in another crate. The giant returned to his natural state, too weakened to maintain the form of a whirlwind, and fell backwards onto the floor. Laticus was on him in an instant and was easily able to slice off the last head, which he put into a crate. He then took his sword, ran it through the giant's heart, and crashed to the floor in total exhaustion.

X. The reign restored

Torne la regina

Il ritorno della regina

Fossor the gardener had been listening in terror to the sounds of battle that had been coming from the upper level of the castle. When the noises ceased, he feared the worst and hid behind a tree outside the castle. He was sure that the giant would emerge from the castle in a rage, destroy everything in sight and go on a killing spree. The gardener remained hidden behind the tree for some time. After hearing absolutely nothing for quite a while, he decided to stealthily enter the castle to investigate. He was certain that he would find the remains of Laticus scattered all over the upper floor of the castle. How shocked he was when he peeked into the giant's dining room and saw the giant, headless and with a sword in his heart.

When Fossor saw Laticus he immediately ran to him and poured some cool water on his forehead. Laticus awoke but could hardly move. Fossor saw the key to the prison in the cellar hanging from the giant's belt, and he removed it and immediately ran down into the cellar and liberated the people who had been enslaved. His own family members were among them, and there was great jubilation at their emancipation. Fossor told the people what had happened and they began to sing Laticus's praises. They then began to run through the village to proclaim the good news to all the inhabitants and tell them that they could come out of the caves and cellars where they had been hiding for nearly two years.

Fossor the gardener returned to the upper floor and found Laticus placing his seven golden apples into a large sack. Laticus and Fossor then took the seven crates containing the seven heads of the giant and threw them into the fireplace one by one. The two men stared at the fire until all seven crates were nothing but ashes, and then Fossor said to Laticus, "Wait here. I will return shortly." In a short while, he returned with twenty strong servants. He then said to them, "Please hoist the body of the giant, throw it out the window, and bury it somewhere on the side of the mountain. Then, please come back and clean up the bloody mess in this room. The queen will not be able to move back into her castle if it looks like this!" The men immediately began the difficult task of disposing of the giant's body. Fossor then turned to Laticus and said, "Sir, it is time for you to meet the queen. But first we need to get you cleaned up and find you a set of clothes fit for a prince."

Word of the giant's death spread very quickly through the village and surrounding areas, and people began to come out of their hiding places to celebrate their freedom. The news also reached the queen, and she and her daughter also came out of hiding. They were immediately escorted to the castle that they had been forced to evacuate when the Giant with Seven Heads began terrorizing the land. The queen was pleased to see that her servants had already begun cleaning up the castle and removing every trace of the Giant with Seven Heads, but at the same time she felt guilty because she knew that not only the castle but just about every house in the village needed restoration after the giant's reckless, vandalous behavior. She was about to tell the servants to stop working on the castle and to go and help

the townspeople restore their damaged houses when one of the maidservants approached her. "Your Majesty," she said "it would mean so much to us all if you went straight to the throne room and occupied your throne again. It would be a very important symbolic gesture that would show that our queendom belongs to us again." All the servants in the vicinity smiled and nodded their agreement.

Queen Fausta was very touched by the words of her maidservant. She ceremoniously walked into the throne room. She gazed solemnly at her throne for a moment and then slowly ascended it and sat down. Her daughter took her rightful place at the queen's right hand. All the servants who had been working on restoring the castle made their way into the throne room. Their faces radiated a joyous solemnity at the sight of their beloved queen and princess seated on their thrones again. It was indeed a solemn moment. Most of the maidservants were weeping with joy

After a short while the queen stood up and said, "That is enough solemnity. I would now like to meet the brave young man who has slain the giant and liberated us from tyranny. Will someone please have him brought to me?" Several of the servants, most of whom had been imprisoned in the cellar during the giant's cruel reign, ran out of the throne room to fetch Laticus. It was at this very moment that Fossor the gardener was escorting Laticus down the stairs that led from the upper level of the castle into the foyer. Laticus was feeling clean and fresh and was dressed in a fine garment. He was looking forward to meeting the queen and was very curious what she would be like. When the servants saw Laticus they hoisted him onto their shoulders and jubilantly carried him to the queen. A red carpet had been rolled out to him in front of the queen's throne. Laticus walked down the red carpet and knelt before the queen, who stepped down from her throne and lowered a sword onto his shoulder as a sign of honorary knighthood. It was then that Laticus's eyes met those of the queen's daughter Lina, and he immediately fell in love with her. "A more beautiful girl I have never seen," he thought.

Laticus stood up, thanked the queen for the honor that had been bestowed upon him, and began to tell his story to all those present. He told them all about Pumaria and all the adventures that had brought him to the Valley of the Giant with Seven Heads. He dramatized his story as much as possible in order to impress the princess, who listened very attentively and blushed and smiled every time her eyes met Laticus's. The queen, who also listened attentively to Laticus's story, was of course not blind to what was going on between Laticus and her daughter. When Laticus had finished his story, the queen said, "I think that a fine young prince like you who has done our queendom such a great service would be an excellent husband to my daughter. What do you say, Lina?" Lina immediately gave her consent. Laticus was overjoyed.

The next day, the queen called the residents of the town together in the marketplace and made some important announcements. "My dear people," she said, "because of the years of occupation by the Giant with Seven Heads, much of our land has been destroyed or badly neglected. It will take a while to restore the houses and buildings to their original beauty, but work will begin immediately. Our castle, where the giant has dwelt, also needs a lot of renovation, but work will not begin on the castle until all of you are back in your

homes." This brought many cheers from the townspeople. "Furthermore," said Queen Fausta, "in the dining room of the castle where the Giant with Seven Heads was slain a statue of Laticus is to be erected and a large plaque mounted at its base that recounts the story of how he slew the giant. And by the way, Laticus and Lina are to be wed." This last announcement caused the townspeople to again erupt in cheers and applause.

XI. Dilemma
'Nu dubbiu
Un dubbio

Laticus and Lina were soon married. At first, Laticus felt so much excitement in his wonderful new life that it was not terribly difficult for him to repress his homesickness for Pumaria. There was so much going on to distract him, and there were many buildings throughout the valley that had been damaged by the rampages of the giant and that needed restoration. Because Laticus was knowledgeable in the art of construction, he was very helpful to the queen during this period and worked right alongside her carpenters and masons.

After a year had passed and life had become more tranquil for Laticus and Lina, Laticus began to become more and more nostalgic and to dream incessantly of his homeland. He dreamed of his family and friends, and imagined that they must have given him up for dead by now. The thought of his mother in mourning saddened him very much. He thought of Eliades, the old man whom he had met when he first entered the Valley of the Giant with Seven Heads and who had told him that he would help him return home if he was successful in slaying the giant. Laticus decided to return to the forest where he had met Eliades and search for him. He searched everywhere for hours but could not find him. He thought that if he could find some of the strange animals with human faces he could ask them the whereabouts of Eliades, but he could not find any of them either. He then decided to explore the possibility of returning to Pumaria the way he had come, that is, by climbing up the long rope on which he had been lowered into the tunnel. He said to himself, "My father and brothers completely unraveled the rope when they lowered me into the great hole, but the tip of the rope should still be nailed to the spool. The question is whether the rope and nail will still hold my weight after being exposed to the weather and elements for so long."

Laticus walked through the forest and found his way to the chamber where he had wrested the sword from the hand of the bronze warrior and opened the door to the Valley of the Giant with Seven Heads. The great iron door was still open and Laticus entered the chamber. He looked up the tunnel and saw that the rope still extended upward into the darkness. He grasped the rope and started to climb upwards, but after he had climbed only ten feet or so his weight caused the rope to come loose from the spool far above and he plummeted to the floor. In order to avoid being crushed by the long, heavy rope that plunged down the tunnel he let go of the rope and quickly rolled out of the way. Clearly, he was not going to return home in this way.

Laticus thought things over for a while and concluded that the queen was his only hope. "The queen is wise and resourceful," thought Laticus. "She will know how to get me home or at least how to find Eliades." But when Laticus started going over in his mind exactly how he would word his request to the queen, he began to realize how delicate the matter was and that the queen might very well forbid Laticus to return to Pumaria. "If I tell Queen Fausta that I want to return to Pumaria without Lina," he reasoned, "she might

forbid it because she will not want her daughter's heart to be broken. But if I say that I want to return to my homeland with Lina at my side, she might again forbid it because the loss of her daughter would break her heart."

After long deliberation, Laticus decided that the only sensible thing to do was to talk to his wife. "Lina," he said to her, "I love you more than anything in this world and am very happy to be your husband. It would grieve my heart so if I were to be separated from you. But sometimes my heart aches so much for my homeland that I cannot bear the sadness. I want to go home but do not know how to get there. If I ever discovered how to get there I would never want to leave you behind. Please tell me what you think I should do." Lina was young but had learned wisdom and kindness from her mother. "My dear husband and savior of my country," she said to Laticus, "I have been expecting this moment for some time now, and have had plenty of time to think about how to answer the question that I knew would come. I am certain that you are very saddened because you miss your family. But there is something else that saddens you even more than being separated from your family and that is the knowledge that your family and friends are grieving your death unnecessarily. You would feel much less sadness if you could just let them know that you are alive, well and happy. In order to do this you must find a way to return to Pumaria. I would insist on going with you. After all that you have told me about your kingdom, your family and your friends, I am just as anxious to go there as you are. And, I know that once you are back in your homeland, you will not want to leave it soon. The only solution to our dilemma is to find a way to divide our time between your country and mine."

When Laticus heard these words he nearly wept for joy because he realized more than ever that he had been blessed with the best wife that any man could ask for. "Lina," he said, "I am truly a fortunate man. Will you accompany me to your mother and help me persuade her to help us find a way to travel to Pumaria?" Lina of course agreed to Laticus's request and together they went before Lina's mother the queen, who was conversing with some of the townspeople. Laticus asked the queen for permission to talk to her, saying that he had something very important to discuss with her. She interrupted her conversation with the townspeople and asked him to proceed.

After Laticus had laid forth his proposal to Queen Fausta and humbly asked for her help, he was astounded and amazed that the queen answered him with almost exactly the same words that Lina had used when Laticus asked her what she thought he should do. "My dear son-in-law and savior of my queendom," said the queen, "I have been expecting this moment for some time now, and have had plenty of time to think about how to answer the question that I knew would come. Your need to go home is great not only because you miss your family and friends, but because you cannot bear the thought that they are unnecessarily grieving your death. I would be a horrible tyrant and ingrate if I refused to allow the rescuer of my country to return home, and I would be terribly cruel if I brought about the separation of my daughter from the man whom she so dearly loves. Your idea of dividing your time between this land and yours is a just compromise. I accept it whole-heartedly."

The queen noticed the look of amazement on Laticus's face and asked him what it was that he found so astonishing. Laticus answered, "Your Majesty, when I approached

your daughter on this matter, she answered me using almost exactly the same words and line of reasoning that you have used. You have clearly passed on many wonderful traits to her. In my country, when children take after one of their parents, we say, 'The apple does not fall far from the tree,' and Lina is certainly a good example of this. She is truly a *golden apple* that has fallen from a golden apple tree." The queen laughed and said with a twinkle in her eye, "I suppose that if you are from a country called Pumaria you will naturally resort to expressions involving apples." Everyone in the room laughed heartily at the queen's sense of humor, and then the queen said to one of her stewards, "Send out word through the entire valley that the old animal keeper named Eliades is to be brought before me immediately. Tell him that a prince and princess need his help."

XII. Journey to Pumaria
Viaggiu a Pumaria
Viaggio a Pumaria

After a week or so of searching, Eliades was found in a secluded part of the forest and brought to the castle. He was brought to a room where Queen Fausta, Prince Laticus and Princess Lina were waiting. Laticus said, "Eliades, it is so good to see you again. You were the first person that I met in this valley." Eliades answered, "It is nice to see you again too, brave young prince. I was wondering when nostalgia for your homeland would cause you to ask for my assistance." Laticus said, "I have the queen's permission to travel to my country, and you did mention to me that I should talk to you when the time came for me to go home. By the way, I have returned a few times to the forest where I first encountered you but have not seen any of the timid animals with the human-like faces. Where are they?" Eliades answered, "When the giant died the curse was lifted and the animals became human again. They have left the forest and have returned to the places where they used to live." "That is good to know," said Laticus. "But you remained in the forest nonetheless." "Once a hermit, always a hermit", answered Eliades. "And besides, there are other animals in the forest to tend to."

Laticus then began to ask Eliades how he and Lina could travel to Pumaria. "If you want to go back to your kingdom," said Eliades, "you must do exactly as I tell you. First, you must find a goat and slaughter it. The meat of the goat should be boiled and then salted, and the pelt tanned. Then, you must make a sack out of the pelt and stitch it together in such a way that it has two compartments. The bigger the sack, the better. One compartment must be filled with the meat of the goat and the other with water. For yourself and the princess, a large flask of water will suffice, since your journey to Pumaria will not take long. When you have prepared the goat-skin and the supply of meat and water, I will accompany you to the top of a tall hill a half day's journey from here. From time to time, a giant eagle lands on top of that hill. Because I am the keeper of the animals for this land, the eagle will recognize me and he will allow you and your princess to mount him. While the eagle is flying you to your kingdom, he will sometimes ask for meat or water, which you are to take from the goat-skin sack and give to him. However, be careful, because when he asks for meat, you are to give him water, and when he asks for water, you are to give him meat."

Laticus was full of questions. "Why do we have to give him water when he asks for meat and meat when he asks for water? Why doesn't he just ask for what he wants? Isn't it kind of dangerous to be flying around on a giant eagle? What if he tries to eat *us*? And how will he know how to reach my kingdom?" Eliades replied, "When I first met you, you could not stop asking questions, and I see that you haven't changed since I last saw you. But there is no time for questions now. You must have faith in me and get down to your tasks." Laticus then suddenly remembered the giant bird that he had once seen while wandering through the mountains near his home, and he wondered…...

Laticus and Lina followed the directions of Eliades precisely and in two days were

ready to go with him to the top of the hill. But first, they had to bid farewell to the people in the valley. This was a bittersweet experience for Laticus. He was very anxious to go home to his family, but at the same time he knew that he would badly miss the many friends he had made in his new home. The queen refused to allow herself to become emotional. "I know that you will not forget us and that you will come back to see us often," she said to Laticus and Lina. And then they parted with Eliades, carrying a goat-skin sack full of meat and water, a flask of water for themselves, and a sack containing the seven golden apples. "If we are fortunate," Laticus said to Lina, "we will arrive in Pumaria before the end of the *sacra du pumu*. That would be a wonderful way for you to spend your first days in my kingdom."

Laticus, Lina and Eliades had not been waiting long when the giant eagle arrived. Even though Laticus had only caught a brief glimpse of the giant bird that he had seen some years before in the mountains near his castle, he was sure that this was the same bird, and he felt relieved. "I believe that this eagle knows how to get to my kingdom," he said to Lina and Eliades, "for he has been there before." When the eagle landed, he at first seemed very un-approachable and dangerous as he perched on a large rock, but Eliades bravely walked right up to him and began to speak to him. "You are to carry these two to a kingdom bounded only by treacherous mountains and the sea, with rivers flowing through it and where apple trees abound." He then bade Laticus and Lina to mount the eagle. Laticus climbed onto the eagle's back and sat down right behind his head. Lina sat right behind Laticus. The goatskin sack, the water flask and the sack containing the seven golden apples were all strapped to Laticus's body. As the eagle spread his wings and was about to take off, Laticus asked Eliades if he would allow him just one more question. "Of course," Eliades replied. "What do we have to do if we want to return to this country for a visit?" asked Laticus. "That is easy," said Eliades. "All you have to do is return to the spot where the eagle sets you down and wait. He will soon return there and bring you back here." Upon that, Eliades gave a sign, and the eagle was off.

Laticus and Lina had not been airborne for very long when the eagle started to screech his wishes. "Water!" "Water!" "Meat!" "Meat!" If the eagle asked for water, Laticus would reach into the goatskin sack, take out some meat, reach forward and place it in the eagle's beak. If the eagle asked for meat, Laticus would open the compartment of the goatskin sack containing water, hold it up to the eagle's beak, and pour some water in. Everything seemed to go fine. They flew over dense forests and high mountains. They saw no sign of civilization. Laticus could see that the mountains were indeed treacherous and impassable and he was glad that he had never ventured very far into them.

After they had been in flight for some time, Laticus could feel that the goatskin sack had become very light, and he began to grow concerned about what might happen if they ran out of provisions for the eagle. Laticus began to take heart when he saw in the far, far distance what looked like the sea. He knew that they could not be far from their destination. At this point the eagle screeched for more water. Laticus reached his hand into the meat compartment and discovered to his great dismay that it was empty! "What should I do?" he asked Lina. Lina did not know what to tell him. They were not prepared for this turn of events. "Since you have no more meat, why not just give him water and see what happens?" she suggested in a whisper. Laticus followed her advice and poured some wa-

ter from the sack into the beak of the eagle. The eagle immediately spit the water out and screeched even louder, "Water! Water! Water!" Laticus and Lina could do nothing. The eagle then started to screech even louder for water. To make matters even worse, he began to fly recklessly and to show signs that he might just turn around and go back. Laticus and Lina were genuinely afraid of falling off the eagle's back.

Laticus again looked at the sea in the far distance and decided that they had come too far and were too close to their destination for him to allow anything to go wrong. He decided that he would have to do something drastic. He unsheathed his sword. "What are you going to do?" asked Lina in a terrified voice. Laticus did not answer her. Instead, he quickly sliced off a piece of the calf of his right leg. Lina screamed. The eagle jolted in the air and Laticus and Lina nearly lost their hold. Laticus nearly fainted from the pain and shock, but he found the strength to lean forward and place this piece of his own bloody flesh into the beak of the eagle. The eagle took the meat but could sense that it was not of animal origin and therefore did not swallow it. He simply held it in his beak for a few moments. He then took the piece of Laticus's calf in his left talon, reached around to his right side and placed the flesh back onto Laticus's leg. The flesh stuck to the leg and the wound miraculously healed instantly. The eagle seemed to realize that Laticus's bravery had been tested enough and that he now really deserved to go home.

After a while the eagle began to descend into the mountains. In order to avoid being seen by anyone in the Kingdom of Pumaria, he landed in a valley just beyond the foothills and mountains, not too far from the castle, and set the couple down. Laticus recognized the spot as the one where he had once seen the eagle years before. The eagle then spoke to Laticus in a high-pitched squawk. "If you want to return to the valley whence we have come, the land ruled by Queen Fausta, you need only come to this spot and wait. I will know your wishes and will return here to fetch you." Laticus replied, "Thank you for your kindness. And by the way, it is very nice to hear you say something other than 'Meat' or 'Water' for a change!" The eagle then squawked a friendly laugh and said, "Forgive my final test of your bravery. I will see you again." And with that he spread his wings and took off at incredible speed. He was out of sight in an instant.

XIII. Home

Alla casa

A casa

Laticus and Lina made their way up the side of the mountain and down again the other side. They then walked through the foothills and before long they found themselves on the castle lawn. It was late afternoon and the sun was low and bright. The sight of the castle and its surroundings bathed in sunlight sent Laticus's heart soaring. Lina, sensing his rapture, also felt a sense of elation such as she had never felt before. But then Laticus halted suddenly and a somber look came upon his face. "What is the matter, my love?" Lina asked. Laticus answered softly, "The lawn in front of the castle is empty. There is no *sacra du pumu*. This is a bad sign." They then continued to walk towards the castle.

One of the servant girls who happened to be looking out the window saw the couple approaching. At first she thought she was dreaming, but as soon as she realized that it was Laticus she ran screaming with joy to the king and queen. "Laticus has returned with a beautiful girl!" The king and queen, Laticus's six brothers and their families and all the servants in the castle ran down to the lawn to meet the approaching couple. Laticus knew that it was his mother the queen whom he would embrace before all others. She held her son so tightly that he could hardly breathe and she wept profusely, but she was beside herself with joy.

After Laticus had greeted everyone and introduced them to Lina, everyone began begging Laticus to tell them about what had happened since that fateful day when he was lowered on a rope into the deep, dark hole without a cowbell. "I will tell you everything," Laticus said, "but first you must tell me why you are not celebrating the *sacra du pumu*. Has the harvest not been successful?" King Giuseppe stepped forward. "My son," he said, "we have in fact had very successful harvests since your disappearance. The reason why we are not celebrating the sacra is quite simply that after the loss of the seven golden apples and, more importantly, the loss of our beloved Prince Laticus, no one in the kingdom has had any desire to celebrate anything anymore." "Well, I am back now," said Laticus, "so we should immediately start celebrating the apple festival. But first, there is something very important that must be done. Please come with me into the inner court of the castle."

Everyone followed Laticus as he walked towards the inner court with a mysterious bag in one hand and Lina`s hand in the other. He walked right up to the tree where the seven golden apples had once hung. He waited until everyone had reached the spot where he was standing, and then he said, "My dear family and loyal friends, behold!" He then took the seven golden apples out of the sack one by one. He handed three of them to Lina, who held two in one hand and one in the other. Laticus held two apples in each hand. Lina and Laticus both raised their arms as high as they could so that everyone could see the seven golden apples. The apples reflected the light of the setting sun and shone so bright that they seemed to be seven little golden suns. Laticus's family and all the servants gasped in awe and wonder and then they burst into uncontrolled cheering and jubilation. The Kingdom

of Pumaria had never known a more joyous day. Laticus then asked his brother Zoticus, who had fully recovered from his injuries, if he would climb the tree and reattach the apples to the places that they had occupied before they were stolen by the dreadful Giant with Seven Heads. Zoticus took the seven golden apples from Laticus and Lina. A feeling of solemnity overcame everyone as he attached the golden apples one by one to their respective branches. As he came back down from the tree the sun was about to disappear behind the castle walls, but for a final few moments it shone on the golden apples and created a beautiful, sparkling, golden spectacle. When the sun had gone out of view, King Giuseppe gave an order. "Tomorrow afternoon we will begin the biggest *sacra du pumu* that the kingdom has ever known. After we have eaten and drunk our fill, Laticus will tell us about his journey and about how he was able to retrieve our seven golden apples. Now, I think that maybe he and his beautiful bride would like to be shown to their quarters."

The following day there was indeed a splendid celebration with food, drink, singing and dancing. Undoubtedly the most exciting part of the celebration was the recounting by Laticus of everything that had happened to him since his descent into the mysterious hole. He spoke for many hours, late into the night, but his audience was spellbound and no one said a word.

Laticus and Lina settled in Pumaria and raised their own family there. You can rest assured that they made many journeys on the back of the giant eagle back and forth between Pumaria and the former Valley of the Giant with Seven Heads, and that they lived happily ever after.